Swan in Love

To Ed
—E. B.

To the voice that directs me from within
—J. M. S.

Atheneum Books for Young Readers
An imprint of Simon & Schuster Children's Publishing Division
1230 Avenue of the Americas
New York, New York 10020
Text copyright © 2000 by Eve Bunting
Illustrations copyright © 2000 by Jo Ellen McAllister Stammen
All rights reserved, including the right of reproduction in whole or in part in any form.
Book design by Angela Carlino
The text of this book is set in Deepdene
The illustrations are rendered in pastel
Printed in Hong Kong
10 9 8 7 6 5 4 3 2
Library of Congress Cataloging-in-Publication Data
Bunting, Eve, 1928-
Swan in love / by Eve Bunting; illustrated by Jo Ellen McAllister Stammen.—1st ed.
p.   cm.
Summary: Despite the ridicule of the other animals, Swan persists in his adoration for a
swan-shaped boat named Dora.
ISBN 0-689-82080-1
[1. Swans—Fiction. 2. Boats and boating—Fiction. 3. Animals—Fiction.]
I. McAllister Stammen, Jo Ellen, ill. II. Title.
PZ7.B91527Sw   1999   [e]—dc21   98-7906

Swan in Love

written by EVE BUNTING

illustrated by JO ELLEN McALLISTER STAMMEN

ATHENEUM BOOKS FOR YOUNG READERS

On the lake was a boat shaped like a swan. Her name, DORA, was printed in black on her sparkling paint.

Swan loved her.

In spring and summer when people rode in the boat, Swan followed.
"How cute!" the people said. Sometimes they threw him bread crumbs.

Once a hand, soft as neck down, reached out to stroke his feathers. Swan had never felt anything so comforting.

The other swans muttered among themselves. "He makes us look stupid. Doesn't he know she's not one of us?"

Swan knew. He knew that it didn't matter.

The fish laughed their silvery laughs. "Swan's in love. Doesn't he know she's different?"

Swan knew. He knew that difference makes no difference to love.

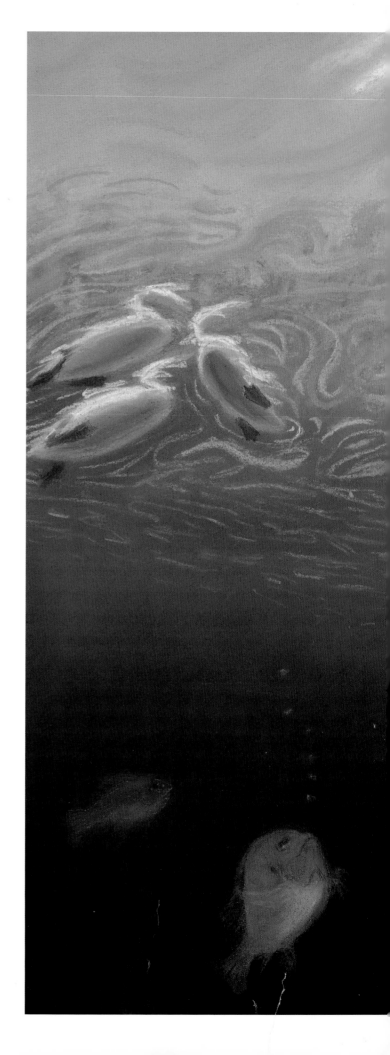

The frogs who lived in the thin lake reeds croaked, "This is wrong, wrong, wrong!"

Swan heard. He knew that love was never wrong.

Sometimes at night an opossum tiptoed down to drink the lake water.
"It would be wiser if you gave your love to another swan," she said.

Swan listened politely. He knew that love wasn't always wise.

He bobbed on the water next to Dora, happy there with only the floating moon between them.

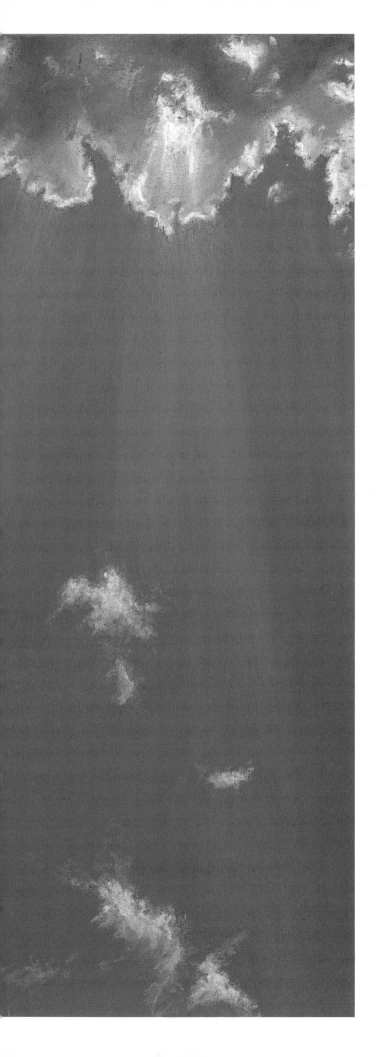

There were times when Swan heard another mysterious voice . . . not a swan, not a fish, not a frog, not an opossum.

"Don't ever stop loving," it said.

Swan thought it came from the sky, or the lake, or the air itself. The voice was a friend.

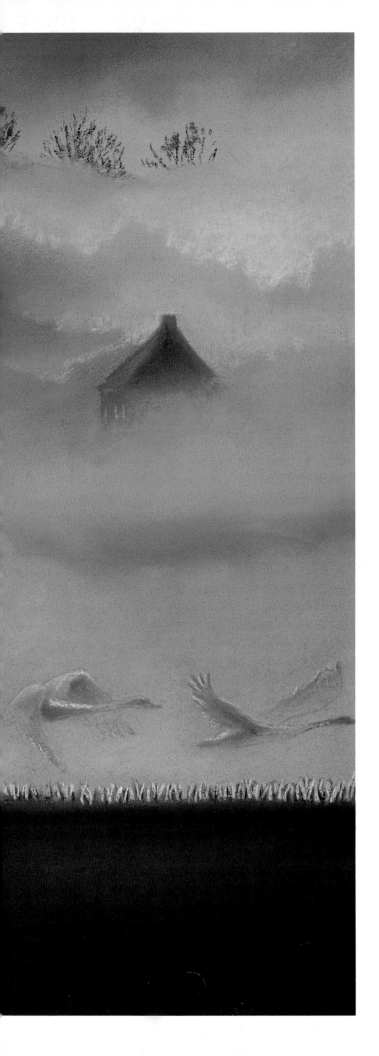

In winter, when the lake clinked with floating ice, the man who owned the swan boat came to pull her out of the water. "See you in spring, Dora," he said.

Then Swan lay, day and night, on the frosted grass beside her.

The other swans left.

The fish and the frogs dived below the ice to hide till the weather changed.

Opossum stayed warm in her den.

Canada geese came.

"That silly Swan is still here," they honked. "Imagine!"

They rested on the ice, then rose again below the clouds.

"Come with us," they called. "We'll fly slowly. We'll help you find your friends. Winter is long, and you will be alone."

"Thank you," Swan said. "But I won't be alone." He tucked his head beneath his wing.

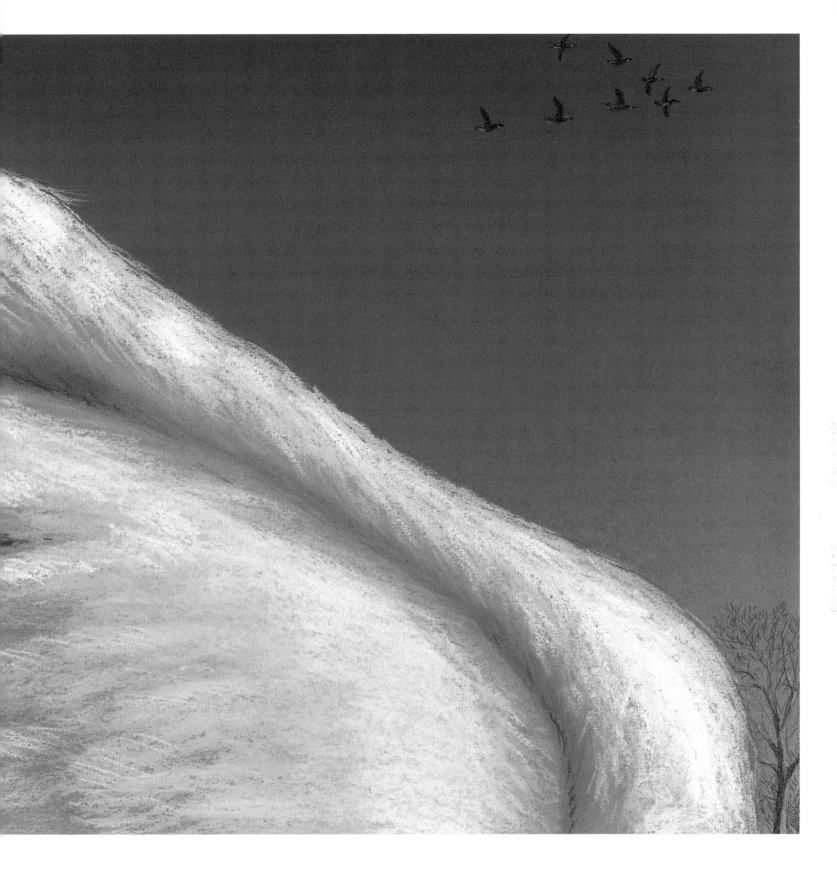

Winters did seem longer and colder every year. He was stiffer than he'd
once been. Slower.

And Dora? Cracks, thin as spiders' webs, veined her body. Her white gleam had turned to the gray of lake pebbles.

In winter, the voice spoke to him through the pale sunshine or starlit wind.

"Faithful Swan," it said. "You have found the answer."

Swan didn't understand. But the voice warmed him.

One spring the man came, fat as a bear in his bundle of a coat.

"You're not looking good, old girl," he told Dora, nudging her off the shore and onto the lake.

Swan flapped in beside her.

Trickles of water streamed through Dora's cracks.

"Oh my!" the man said. "I've got to get you out of there before you sink like a rock." His great rubber boots squelched mud as he dragged her back out.

Swan's heart beat thick in his breast. Dora!

The man kicked gently at her sides. A crack widened.

"Poor old thing," he said. "Looks like there's nothing we can do for you. I'll come back in a day or two and break you up. Hate to do it but . . ."

Swan fluttered out of the lake, hissing and spitting. He bit at the big rubber boot.

The man fended him off. "Okay, now! Take it easy, fellow. I know how you feel and I'm sorry. But our Dora's finished. And you don't look so good yourself."

Swan hunched over next to Dora,
listening as the man's truck roared
away, listening to the silence of their
lake.

Finished!

He drifted through waves of time,
his body light as mist, and he heard
the voice, soft and comforting as that
hand that had once stroked his
feathers.

"Love makes magic," it said.

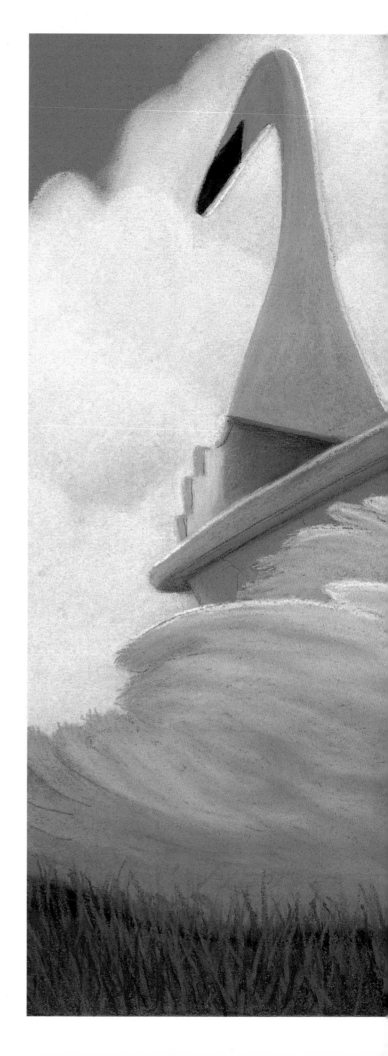

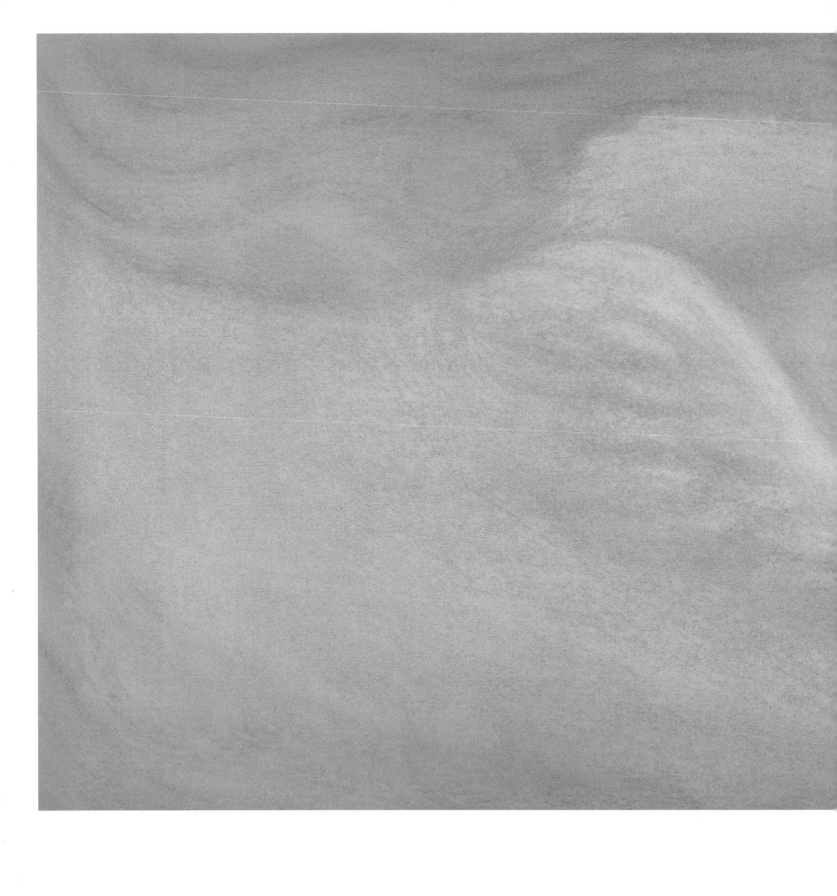

There was a flowing then, a streaming against Swan's folded wings, and he was somewhere, Dora beside him.

But she wasn't Dora though he knew she was. And he wasn't Swan though he knew he was.

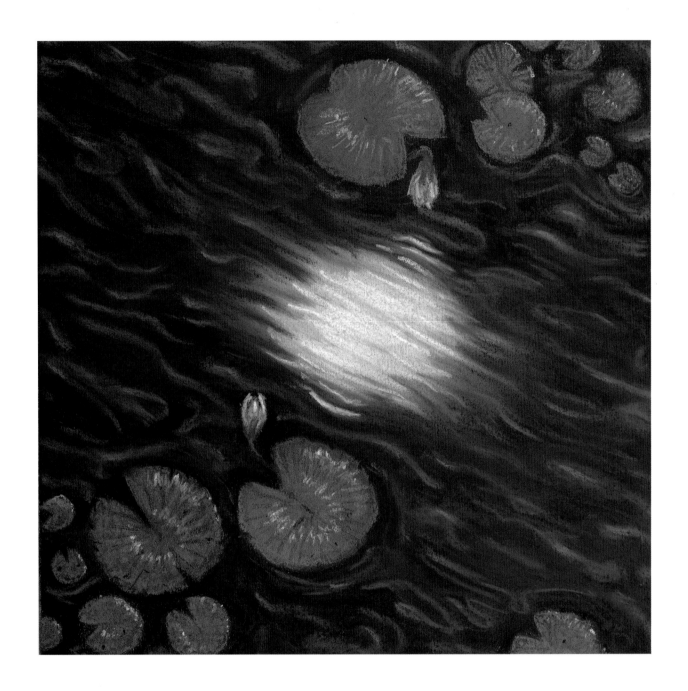

Love makes magic, he thought, and he looked down from a distance and saw them, two water lilies resting quietly on the lake, nothing between them but the floating moon.